THE FAMOUS FIVE
SHORT STORIES

MESSAGE IN A BOTTLE

The Famous Five

Timmy   George   Julian   Dick   Anne

HODDER CHILDREN'S BOOKS

First published in Great Britain in 2023 by Hodder & Stoughton

For further information about the editorial history of this book, see enidblyton.co.uk/books

3 5 7 9 10 8 6 4 2

The Famous Five®, Enid Blyton® and Enid Blyton's signature
are registered trade marks of Hodder & Stoughton Limited
Written by Sufiya Ahmed. Text © 2023 Hodder & Stoughton Limited
Illustrations by Becka Moor. Illustrations © 2023 Hodder & Stoughton Limited

A CIP catalogue record for this book is available from the British Library.

ISBN 978 1 444 96710 4

Printed and bound in China
The paper and board used in this book are made from wood from responsible sources.

Hodder Children's Books
An imprint of
Hachette Children's Group
Part of Hodder & Stoughton
Carmelite House
50 Victoria Embankment
London EC4Y 0DZ

An Hachette UK Company
www.hachette.co.uk
www.hachettechildrens.co.uk

Enid Blyton

Message in a Bottle

illustrated by **Becka Moor**

written by **Sufiya Ahmed**

HODDER

Famous Five Colour Short Stories

Five and a Half-Term Adventure

George's Hair Is Too Long

Good Old Timmy

A Lazy Afternoon

Well Done, Famous Five

Five Have a Puzzling Time

Happy Christmas, Five!

When Timmy Chased the Cat

The Birthday Adventure

Five to the Rescue!

Timmy and the Treasure

Five and the Runaway Dog

Message in a Bottle

For a complete list of the full-length
Famous Five adventures, turn to
the last page of this book

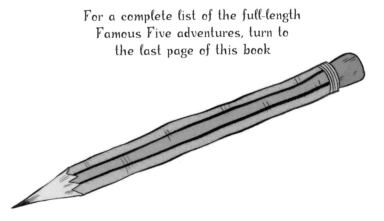

CONTENTS

CHAPTER ONE — page 1

CHAPTER TWO — page 11

CHAPTER THREE — page 21

CHAPTER FOUR — page 31

CHAPTER FIVE — page 41

CHAPTER SIX — page 53

CHAPTER SEVEN — page 63

CHAPTER ONE

'**Catch!**' Anne shouted, throwing the ball in the air.

Timmy **jumped up** and caught it, returning to Anne with **his tail wagging.**

Anne turned to her cousin.
'George! Why don't you join us?'

George propped herself up on one elbow. Dick and Julian were sprawled on the blanket beside her. Their tummies were full of **egg sandwiches, meat pie** and **fruit cake.**

'Let me just digest all this **lovely food** first,' she said.

'**Woof!**' Timmy licked Anne's hand. Anne laughed and threw the ball with **extra force.** It **flew up** in the air and landed out of sight. Timmy ran after it, towards the wall along the edge of the field.

A few minutes later, when Timmy had still **not returned,** George got to her feet. '**Why is he taking so long?'**

Anne shielded her eyes from the sun and peered ahead. 'There are some bushes near the wall. Perhaps he's crawled into them.'

'Let's go and see,' George said, **frowning. 'Timmy!'** she called, going after him.

'Woof!'

'I knew it!' Anne said, pointing. **'There he is.'**

'What have you got there, boy?' George asked, getting down on her **hands and knees** to poke her head behind the bush. **'What's this . . .? Oh, look! There's a bottle wedged in the wall.'**

'What do you mean?' asked Anne, **squatting down** beside her.

'It looks as if it's packed in **quite tightly,'** George said.

'Should we disturb it?' Anne wondered in a **slightly worried voice.** 'Someone placed it there for a reason.'

'It looks long-forgotten to me,' George said.

'But—' Anne's objection turned into a surprised squeal as George pulled the bottle out in **one swoop.**

George cleaned a patch of the **filthy** glass with her shirt and held the bottle up.

'There's a piece of paper inside. **We've found a message in a bottle!'**

CHAPTER TWO

Anne, George and Timmy hurried back to
Julian and Dick.

'Look what we found!'

Anne cried. **'A message in a bottle.'**

Julian examined the bottle. 'I wonder what the message is.' He pulled his penknife from his pocket. Slowly and carefully he coaxed the paper through the neck of the bottle. It was **faded and creased** but still intact.

Dick, George and Anne crowded round him, and Timmy **launched** himself on to Julian's lap.

George pulled him away. **'Timmy! Sit!'**

Julian took a **deep breath** and began to read.

Dear Dottie,

I am so sorry that we argued over the doll. I know it belongs to both of us and it was wrong of me to run off with it.

I did come to see you before we move to America, but your mother said you were visiting your grandmother in Devon. I am sad that we didn't get to say goodbye in person.

I have decided to give the doll to you. Although we both won it at the fair, I would like you to keep it as a reminder of our friendship.

I have hidden the doll in the second cave on the mainland shore directly opposite Kirrin Island. She's probably a little wet and cold so be sure to rescue her. And when you play with her, remember me.

Love,

Trinny

'A **secret message** about a doll,' Anne said in wonder. 'Oh, I'd **love** to see what she looked like.'

George smirked. **'You and your dolls.'**

'You don't have to be mean just because you don't play with them,' Anne shot back.

Dick looked **thoughtful**. 'If we found the letter, does that mean Dottie **never did?'**

Julian **carefully** folded the letter and placed it in his back pocket. 'Dottie could have **found** it, **read** it, **put it back** in its place and then **rescued** the doll.'

Anne looked between her brothers. **'Well, which is it?** Did she rescue the doll or not?'

'That's the **mystery,**' Julian said.

'A **mystery** that will be solved by a **cave exploration!**' George declared.

An hour later, the Five **pulled** George's boat along the beach.

'Do you think the cave will be **very dark?**' Anne said in a **worried** voice.

George folded her arms. 'Are you having **second thoughts?**'

'I just don't want to go inside a
creepy cave,' Anne admitted.

'You can **stay on the beach,'** Julian said
in a kind voice. 'We won't be too long.'

Anne looked **relieved.** 'Timmy can stay
with me.'

But **Timmy** had other plans. Turning his back to Anne, he **scrambled** into the boat.

'**You'll regret it, Timmy,**' Anne said, making a face. 'You're always the first one to get spooked.'

'My dog is very brave,'

George said **indignantly**.

Julian and Dick tried to **hide their laughter** and pushed the boat into the sea.

George climbed in and stood at the helm **like a captain,** as Julian and Dick took the oars. '**I'll navigate. I know the way.**'

'Be careful,' Anne said, waving them off, before settling down to read her book.

CHAPTER THREE

Julian and Dick rowed with **all their might.** **'To the left!'** Julian shouted. **'No!'** George spun round to glare down at him. **'The message says "second**

cave on the mainland shore directly opposite Kirrin Island." I know exactly where that is.'

'Better listen to her,' Dick said, huffing as he pulled his oar.

'Faster!' George said.

'Will you be quiet!' Julian snapped. **'It's not easy rowing in choppy water.'**

George **scowled** and turned back round.

They reached the second cave and **slowly** manoeuvred their way inside, losing daylight as they went.

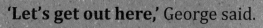

'Let's get out here,' George said.

The three **pulled** the boat up on to a bank. George and Dick **looped** the boat's rope tightly round a **rock.** Julian pulled a torch out of his rucksack. **The light created shadows** that only added to the **spookiness.**

'Woof!' Timmy barked.

His **echo** bounced back, **frightening him.**

He pressed against George's leg and looked up at her **mournfully,** his **tail between his legs.**

'It's all right, boy,' George said soothingly, **patting his head.**

'It's hard getting used to our **echoes,**' Dick said. **'Echo. Echo. Ec—'**

'Stop messing around!' George hissed.

'**Look!**' Julian interrupted the squabble, shining his torch down at the floor of the cave. '**Stone steps have been chiselled here.**'

'That was the work of the **smugglers** many centuries ago,' George announced **excitedly**. 'They used to **hide loot** in these **caves**.'

'Then they must have carved **holes** in the **walls** too,' Julian said, flashing his torch around. 'I think I see one right there.'

'Maybe we'll find some **long-forgotten smugglers' gold,'** Dick said gleefully, climbing the steps to feel inside the gap.

George **snorted.** 'Let's just focus on the **doll.'**

'Eww!' Dick pulled his hand out and shook it, stumbling on the steps. **'It's a home for centipedes.'**

'Come on,' George said, trying **not** to laugh.

CHAPTER FOUR

They moved along, their hands feeling the walls, careful not to **disturb the insects.** After a while, Julian said, 'I don't think it's wise to go too far. **Maybe we should turn back.'**

'Just a little further,' Dick said. 'Think how **happy** Anne would be to see the doll.'

'All right,' Julian agreed, and then **halted.** 'There are more steps here.'

Carefully, he climbed the steps to **point his torch** inside **a large**

square hole. 'I think I see . . .' He paused, and then in a voice full of excitement declared, **'I can see the doll!** She's right here, tucked inside.'

'**Hurrah!**' Dick threw his hands in the air in **victory**.

'I think I can reach her . . .'

But just as Julian **extended his hand**
and made a **grab** for the doll, **his foot
slipped.** He lost his balance and seemed
about to go flying through the air. He **gripped
the rocky wall** and stopped himself falling, but
the **doll flew from his hand.**

It hit the ground with a resounding **crash,** causing the **head** to **break** from the body.

In what seemed like **slow motion,** Julian, Dick and George watched the doll's head **roll slowly forwards** until it stopped right by Timmy's front legs.

Decades of being **crammed** in a **dark cave** meant the doll was not in a pretty state.

Poor Timmy.

Terrified, he turned and **bolted.**

George and Dick **ran** after Timmy, while Julian **grabbed** the **doll's head and body** and **stuffed them** into his rucksack before joining **the chase.** Timmy ran left and right **haphazardly,** taking them deeper into the caves.

When they eventually caught up with him, the children bent over and **clutched their knees,** trying to **catch their breath.**

'Do either of you remember the way we came?' **George panted.**

Julian and Dick glanced at each other worriedly. **They didn't.**

CHAPTER FIVE

Anne closed the pages of her book. **Hours** had passed and there was still no sign of the others.

She scrambled to her knees and **scanned the horizon** for **George's boat.**

She bit her lip. It really was **odd** that they **hadn't returned** yet. **Could something have happened to them?** Anne realised that she needed to **raise the alarm.** Turning round, she ran back to the house **as fast as she could.**

Aunt Fanny was in the living room,
knitting. 'Good, you're in time for dinner,' she
said, and then looked over Anne's shoulder.
'Where are the others?'

'I think they might be **in trouble,**' Anne replied fearfully.

Aunt Fanny's knitting needles **stopped clicking. 'Goodness! What on earth is going on?'**

Julian leant back against the tunnel wall. They had been walking for a while and had still not found their way out. It was like being **in a maze** – the different turnings only seemed to take them **further away** from the entrance. 'I think we're going in the **wrong direction,**' he said.

'Woof!' Timmy barked.

'Are you saying sorry for **running off like a scared rabbit,** Timmy?' Dick said. **'Like this?'**

George rolled her eyes as Dick **jogged on the spot.**

'Stop fooling around,' Julian protested. 'The ground's **slippery** and you'll—'

The warning came too late. Dick's left foot **twisted** and he **crumpled** to the ground.

Julian **flashed his torch** on Dick.

'Are you all right?'

Dick put on a brave face. 'I think so . . .
Actually . . . no . . . I think I've **sprained my
ankle.'**

Timmy **licked** Dick's cheek to
comfort him.

'Put your arm round my shoulder,' Julian said. '**Lean on me** and **hop along.** We need to find our way out or we'll be **trapped all night.'**

'**Maybe for ever,**' Dick joked.

'**It's not the time to be funny!**' George snapped.

Suddenly Julian's torch began to **flicker.** **'Oh, no! The battery's dying.'**

'**Turn it off** and **save it** for when we **really** need it,' George said. 'We can walk in the dark.'

They began to **shuffle along** in the **darkness** with Timmy **whimpering** occasionally. Then Julian **stopped in his tracks,** causing George to bump into Dick.

'**I can see light,**' Julian said. 'It's just a sliver, but it means there's an **opening.**'

Feeling hopeful, they headed towards the light until they were standing in a circle of it.

'It's a dry well,' Julian said, **gazing up.** 'We're at the **bottom** of it and the light is **pouring in** from the top. **Look!** It's **covered with wire mesh to stop people from falling in.**' He felt the wall. 'But it's too smooth. We'll **never** be able to **climb** up.'

'**So we're stuck down here?**' George said.

'Anne knows where we were going,' Julian said. 'She'll **raise the alarm.**'

'At least we solved the **mystery about the letter and the doll,**' Dick said. '**Poor Dottie never found either one.**'

CHAPTER SIX

Anne walked behind the search party. It would be **night** soon and they **still hadn't found the others.**

A **rescue boat** had searched the caves and found **George's moored boat**. The group had now split into two. Some people were searching the caves with George's father, and others were checking out the wells that led down to the caves.

Sergeant Aderemi had brought along a **map** of all the **abandoned wells.**

They were now at the **third** well. Anne leant over it to peer down. There was only darkness below.

'**Julian!**' she shouted desperately. '**Dick! George! Timmy! Bark if you can hear me.**'

'There's no one down there,' Sergeant Aderemi said gently.

Anne's shoulders slumped. She was about to step away when she froze.

'Wait . . .' she said, holding up a hand.

'I can hear something . . . It's a bark! That's Timmy!'

'Oh, thank goodness!' Aunt Fanny exclaimed. 'But where's it coming from?'

Sergeant Aderemi studied his map.

'There's **another well** close to here,' he said. **'Let's go!'**

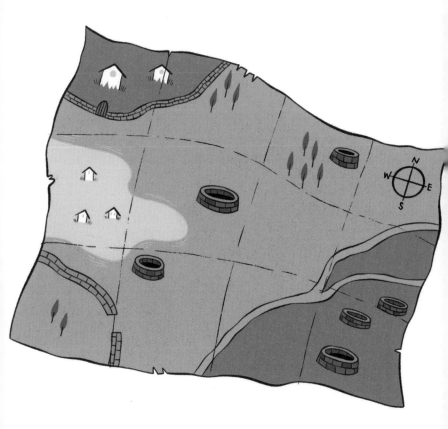

'Timmy!' Dick scolded. '**Stop barking!**'

George sat up. '**Shhhh.** His ears are alert, which means **he can hear something.**'

Timmy looked up. '**Woof!**'

'There must be people up there!'

Julian lurched to his feet.

'Help!' all three shouted together.
'Help!'

A familiar voice shouted down. **'Hello! Lucky I stayed behind!'**

Anne had found them.

A short time later, a wooden ladder was lowered down.

'Climb slowly,' a voice called.

'George, you go first and explain that Dick's hurt,' Julian said. 'He'll need to go up in a crate.'

'What about Timmy?' George asked.

'He can go up with Dick,' Julian promised.

George **patted Timmy's head** and then climbed the ladder.

A wooden crate was soon lowered, and Dick and Timmy climbed in.

'George is up there waiting,' Julian said, **ruffling Timmy's ears.** 'Be a good boy and stay on Dick's lap.'

The crate was pulled up, and then Julian climbed the ladder. When he reached the top, Anne **threw her arms round him.**

Julian grinned at her. **'We found the doll!'**

61

CHAPTER SEVEN

The next morning the Five sat down to a late breakfast.

Julian placed the doll on the table.

He had **screwed the head back on** but she

still looked in a sorry state. **'We solved the mystery,'** he said. 'Dottie never found the note. If she had, **surely** she would have gone looking for the doll.'

'Should we look for **Dottie?'** Anne asked. 'I mean, the doll really **belongs to her,** doesn't it?'

'You're right, Anne,' Aunt Fanny said. 'And I'm proud of you for realising that.'

'But how do we find Dottie?' George asked.

'Why don't you **visit the farms** near where you found the letter?' her mother suggested. 'The owners might know who Dottie was.'

'Good idea,' Dick said as he hobbled to a comfier chair.

'You're not going anywhere with that injured ankle today,' Aunt Fanny said firmly.

Dick's ankle had been examined by the doctor and was now **bandaged.** He slumped in his chair. **'What will I do?'**

Anne picked up the doll. 'I'm going to **mend her clothes, comb her hair** and **clean her up** until she looks new again. **Will you help me, Dick?'**

Dick sighed but agreed.

After breakfast, Julian, George and Timmy visited the nearby farms. They found a woman **feeding her chickens** at the fourth one.

She **listened** to Julian and then **covered her mouth** with her hand. **'I'm Sarah, Dottie's granddaughter.'**

Two days later, the Five waited in the garden of a care home in a neighbouring town. Sarah wheeled **an old lady** to their table.

'Hello, children,' Dottie said. 'My Sarah says you have **something for me.'**

When she had finished reading the letter, Dottie's eyes **filled with tears.**

'I never knew! Trinny was my **best friend** and we used the **bottle in the wall** to leave **messages** for each other. I didn't think to check for another one after she left for **America.'**

Anne stroked Dottie's hand. 'It's all right. You have this now,' she said, handing over the doll.

'She's just like I remember her,' Dottie said, hugging the doll.

'It's lucky you didn't see her yesterday! I worked all morning, cleaning her up,'

Dick said.

After a **sharp look** from his sister, he **blushed** and added, 'Anne showed me how to do it.'

Dottie smiled. **'Thank you, children,** for rescuing my doll. Would you like to stay for tea? They serve **delicious cakes** here.'

'**Timmy** was the one who found the message in the bottle,' George said proudly.

72

'Well then, I think we can find some
dog treats too,' Dottie declared.

Timmy **wagged his tail.** He liked the
sound of that.

If you enjoyed this Famous Five short story, there's plenty more action and adventure in the full-length Famous Five novels. Here is a list of all the titles, in the order they were first published.

1. Five on a Treasure Island
2. Five Go Adventuring Again
3. Five Run Away Together
4. Five Go to Smuggler's Top
5. Five Go Off in a Caravan
6. Five on Kirrin Island Again
7. Five Go Off to Camp
8. Five Get Into Trouble
9. Five Fall Into Adventure
10. Five on a Hike Together
11. Five Have a Wonderful Time
12. Five Go Down to the Sea
13. Five Go to Mystery Moor
14. Five Have Plenty of Fun
15. Five on a Secret Trail
16. Five Go to Billycock Hill
17. Five Get Into a Fix
18. Five on Finniston Farm
19. Five Go to Demon's Rocks
20. Five Have a Mystery to Solve
21. Five Are Together Again